The Manic Panic

RICHA JHA

MITHILA ANANTH

This is what your household looks like on most days.

This is what it will look like the day the Internet stops working.

"What's wrong with the Wi-Fi?" Mommy will howl.

"It's DOWN!" Daddy will bellow.

"Good riddance!" Nana will smirk.

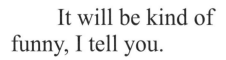

It will be kind of funny, I tell you.

You, on the other hand, will be BRIMMING with ideas and plans for things to do...

...which will be of no use.

"But the Wi-Fi!" they will whine.

This is when you will lose it. You will flare your nostrils, fling your hair, and say what you MUST.

"Mommy! Daddy! BEHAVE! It is NOT the end of the world. The Internet wasn't even around when you were my age."

Their eyes will not blink for a million gazillion seconds.

"But

that

was

THEN..."

they will finally whimper.

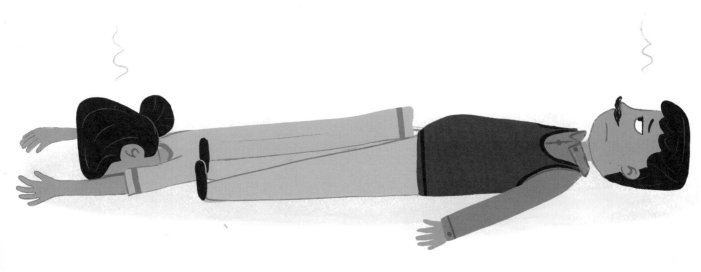

Clearly, you will have to take charge. "Do you see the big wide world out there? Waiting to be explored?" you will ask.

SILENCE.

You will dig in your heels, flex your muscles, and stand firm.

They will grumble.

And fret.

And protest.

But you will
knit your brows,

roll your eyes,

and not give in...

...because YOU know what's good for them.

What fun it will be!

"One last time, PLEASE?" they will plead, as you make your way back home.

HOT TEA HERE

The Wi-Fi will still be down, but now they will have other things to think about.

Like the clouds and the breeze and the trees.

"What a perfect day!" you will sigh and go to your room, tired and happy.

Then you will turn on your computer and FREEZE.

"AHHHHH, my book report!" you'll scream into the quiet night. "Why is the Wi-Fi still down?" you will demand, of no one in particular.

Ask ME.

I should know.

Richa Jha is a picture book author from New Delhi, India. She has been at the receiving end of threats from her two children that one of these days, she might wake up to find her mobile flushed down the toilet. She takes pride in announcing that she is not on Whatsapp.